Dinner
with a
Pirate

A folk tale from Spain

Written by Saviour Pirotta
Illustrated by Shahab Shamshirsaz

 Collins

Pedro was a fisherman and one day
he caught a swordfish.
He thought, "I must share my good
luck with someone."

He made a fish stew and took it to the local prison.

He said to the guard, "I want to share
my food with a prisoner."

Pedro shared his dinner with
a pirate who had been captured.
The pirate ate a lot!

Before Pedro left, the pirate gave him a cheap ring and said, "Thank you for dinner."

Many years later, Pedro was captured
by pirates. He was taken to a country far
away and sold to a rich man.

The rich man came to look at his
new servants. He spotted Pedro's ring
and asked, "Who gave you that?"
"A pirate," Pedro said.

"You must be the fisherman who shared his dinner with me," said the rich man.

"When I came out of prison, I changed my ways. Today I'm an honest man and can repay your kindness. I'll send you home on one of my ships."

"But now, let's have dinner!"

12

13

Dinner with a prisoner

Dinner with a rich man

Ideas for reading

Written by Gillian Howell
Primary Literacy Consultant

Learning objectives: *(reading objectives correspond with Blue band; all other objectives correspond with Ruby band)* read longer words including simple two and three syllable words; use phonics to read unknown or difficult words; deduce characters' reasons for behaviour from their actions; interrogate texts to deepen and clarify understanding and response; develop and refine ideas in writing using planning

Curriculum links: Citizenship: Choices

High frequency words: one, good, with, made, took, want, his, who, had, been, him, many, by, man, came, new, that, must, be, when, out, an, your, home, but, now, have

Interest words: fisherman, swordfish, guard, prisoner, pirate, captured, servants, honest

Resources: paper and pens, collage materials, whiteboard

Word count: 174

Getting started

- Look at the cover and read the title. Point out that this is a folk tale from Spain. Ask the children to say what they already know about folk tales, where they are set and the sort of things that happen in them. Discuss how the folk tales end and elicit that they usually have a moral. Ask them to describe the sort of characters and morals that feature in folk tales and traditional stories.

- Read the back cover blurb. Ask the children to predict what will happen after the fisherman has shared his dinner and explain why, making notes on a whiteboard to return to later.

Reading and responding

- Ask the children to read the story together. Remind them to use their phonic knowledge to work out new words. If they struggle to read "fisherman", ask them to break the word into smaller words or syllables to work it out.

- As they read, pause at significant events, e.g. on p6, ask them to suggest how the pirate feels and why. On p7, and ask them how they think Pedro feels when he's given the cheap ring and compare the two scenes.